My

Book
of

Funny
Valentines

My Book of

Funny Valentines

by Margo Lundell

Illustrated by
Nate Evans

Cartwheel
·B·O·O·K·S·™

SCHOLASTIC INC.
New York   Toronto   London   Auckland   Sydney

Text copyright © 1993 by Margo Lundell.
Illustrations copyright © 1993 by Nate Evans.
All rights reserved. Published by Scholastic Inc.
730 Broadway, New York, NY 10003.
CARTWHEEL BOOKS is a trademark of Scholastic Inc.

ISBN 0-590-44187-6

12 11 10 9 8 7 6 5 4 3 2 1   3 4 5 6 7 8/9
Printed in the U.S.A.   24
First Scholastic printing, January 1993

To Erik Lundell
X X O O
Love, 13 • 15 • 13

To Bren
My Valentine
—N.E.

Part One

Human
Heart to
Heart

Valentine Duet

If you were a flute,
I'd be your sound.
If you were grass,
I'd be the ground.

Wherever you are,
whatever you do,
you'll never be lonely.
I'll be there, too.

The Cranky Gardener

Roses are red,
Violets are blue,
Sugar is sweet,
and so are you.

What do they mean,
"Violets are blue"?
The words may rhyme,
but they're not true.

Purple's common.
White is, too.
But violets
are just not blue.

It's fine if valentines
are trite,
but we should try
to get them right.

Valentine's Day at School

Bully Vinnie,
tall and tough,
said valentines
were stupid stuff.

He brought no silly
cards to pass
to anybody
in his class.

Did *Vinnie* get
a valentine?
He watched as Pete
got eight or nine.

He put his feet up
in the air,
acted bored,
said, "I don't care."

But secretly
he cared a lot
if he got valentines
or not.

Before the afternoon
was through,
thank heavens
Vinnie did get two.

TO: Vinnie

What signatures
did Vinnie find?
The valentines
were left unsigned.

What bully Vinnie
never knew
was that Miss Goodrich
sent those two.

Miss Goodrich says,
and it is true,
that bully boys
have feelings, too.

From the Baby

Let me lie in your lap.
Let me ride on your knee.
Offer all of your kisses
to no one but me.

Hurry and hug me
and snuggle and smile.
I'll only be little
a little while.

Part Two

All Creatures
Care

Squirrel's Song

Acres of acorns,
a million or two,
mean nothing at all.
I'm just nuts over you.

Turtle to His True Love

Down at the pond,
when you swim by,
I always feel
so slow, so shy.

But if you stop
and listen well,
you'll hear a heart
inside this shell.

Happily Married Moles

We ran away
from the world above
and dug ourselves
a tunnel of love.

Sentimental Insect

Two black beetles
cuddled on a rug.
"Oh, hon," said one,
"you're my love bug."

The Story of Catherine and Harry

A pretty cat,
prissy and vain,
was called Miss Kitty
Catherine Jane.

Catherine dressed
from top to toes
in all the best
expensive clothes.

She chose a mate
whose name was Harry.
"You and I,"
she said, "will marry."

"To seal our vow
I now insist,"
said Catherine Jane,
"that I be kissed."

Harry Hanks
was horrified.
"I'm not the kissing kind!"
he cried.

He ran straight home
and hid in bed,
but Catherine followed,
dressed in red.

Harry crouched
behind the stove,
but Catherine came,
all bathed in mauve.

Then Harry climbed
a tree, poor fellow.
Catherine stood below
in yellow.

What to do?
That fancy miss
would wait forever
for her kiss!

Then Harry cried,
"The answer's plain!
I'll fix you, Kitty
Catherine Jane!"

Just down the road
(it wasn't far),
Harry found
a pot of tar.

He hurried back,
all stuck with goo,
and said to Catherine,
"I'll kiss you!"

When Kate saw sticky
Harry Hanks,
she turned his offer
down with thanks.

Way down the street,
she turned and waved.
The life of Harry Hanks
was saved.

Lament of the Bumblebee

Yellow and black,
yellow and black,
please bee mine,
won't you come back?

I never thought
that we would part.
You're gone. You're gone.
I'm stung to the heart.

Part Three

Things
Have
Feelings,
Too!

Plight of a Picture Puzzle

I fell apart today.
It's true.
I went to pieces
over you.

Lovesick Steam Engine

My boiler burst!
My throttle failed!
Because of you
my cars derailed!

The training manual
didn't state
I'd fall in love
with Engine Eight.

What's wonderful
is, I don't care
if I'm in utter
disrepair!

Dear Engine Eight,
I'm in the yard.
Be good enough
to send a card!

The Roots of Love

Once there were
two apple trees
who touched with every
gentle breeze.

Said one, "I love you
to the core.
Your shade, your shape,
and so much more."

The other answered,
seeming shy,
"You are the apple
of my eye."

Poor Violinetta

How did I ruin the concert today?
Violin Vincent led me astray.
Handsome and polished, he smiled at the start.
ZING! went the strings of my violin heart.

"My Hopes All Hinge on You," Says the Door

Don't shut yourself
from me. Be kind.
I beg you, keep
an open mind.

I send this thought
across the floor:
You are the one
that I a-door.

Jacket to Jacket

Lovely cut,
just my size,
made in Spain,
worldly, wise. . . .

Jacket, dear,
I love your weave.
For you, my heart
is on my sleeve.

A Skyscraper Rises
to the Occasion

I gaze upon you,
floor by floor,
and thank my stars
that you're next door.

At dawn each day
we rise and climb.
Let's stand here
for the rest of time.